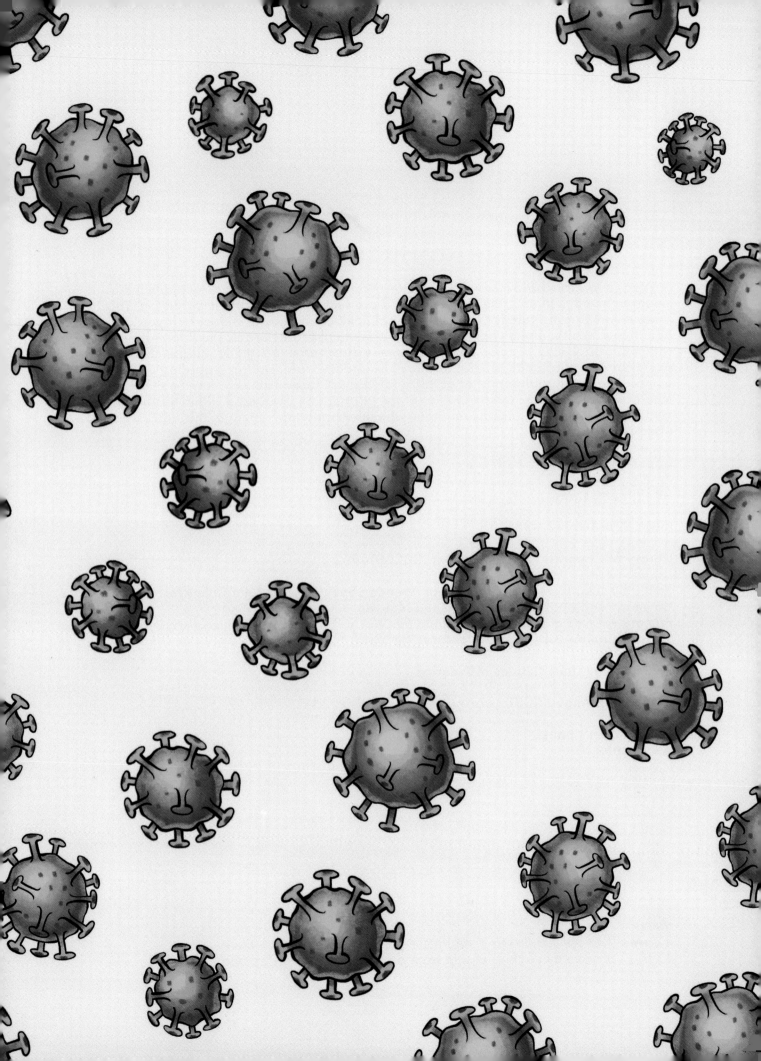

ISBN: 978-1-09833-339-3

Library of Congress Control Number: 2020914982

Edited by Julia Hafer, Deborah Paggi, Brendan Sullivan, and John Calmeyer.
Cover art and book design by Valentin Nguyen.
Primary sources of information include the World Health Organization (WHO) & Centers for Disease Control (CDC). See references for more.

Printed in the United States of America

First Edition August 2020.

MD Children's Books
Los Angeles, CA

Meter:
It **came** / to pla-net **Earth** / and it sur-**prised** / the hu-man **race**,
As **if** / it came by **rock** / et ship from **deep** / dark out-er **space**.

For all those fighting on the front lines.

It came to planet Earth and it surprised the human race,

As if it came by rocket ship from deep, dark outer space.

Its icky sticky fingers hang from grippy grimy hands.

It oozes gobs of goop that spit and splatter when they land.

This creature's microscopic with a sickening persona.

This creature is a virus - and it bears the name Corona.

The virus quickly spread and a new future soon took shape.

It flew across the world wearing its evil virus cape.

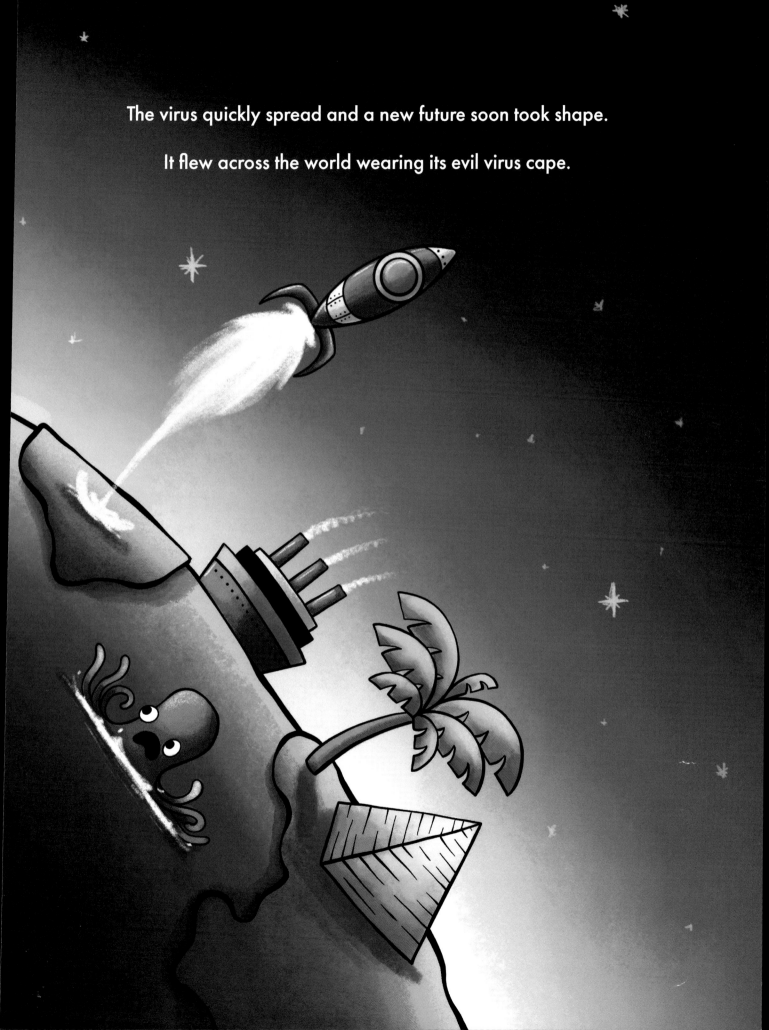

Our tale starts in a world that truly thought it'd seen it all.

To see the bug in *person*, we must shrink down really small.

Come on! Let's climb aboard the Shrink-O-Matic Jet Express.

We'll hop off microscopic - virus size or even less!

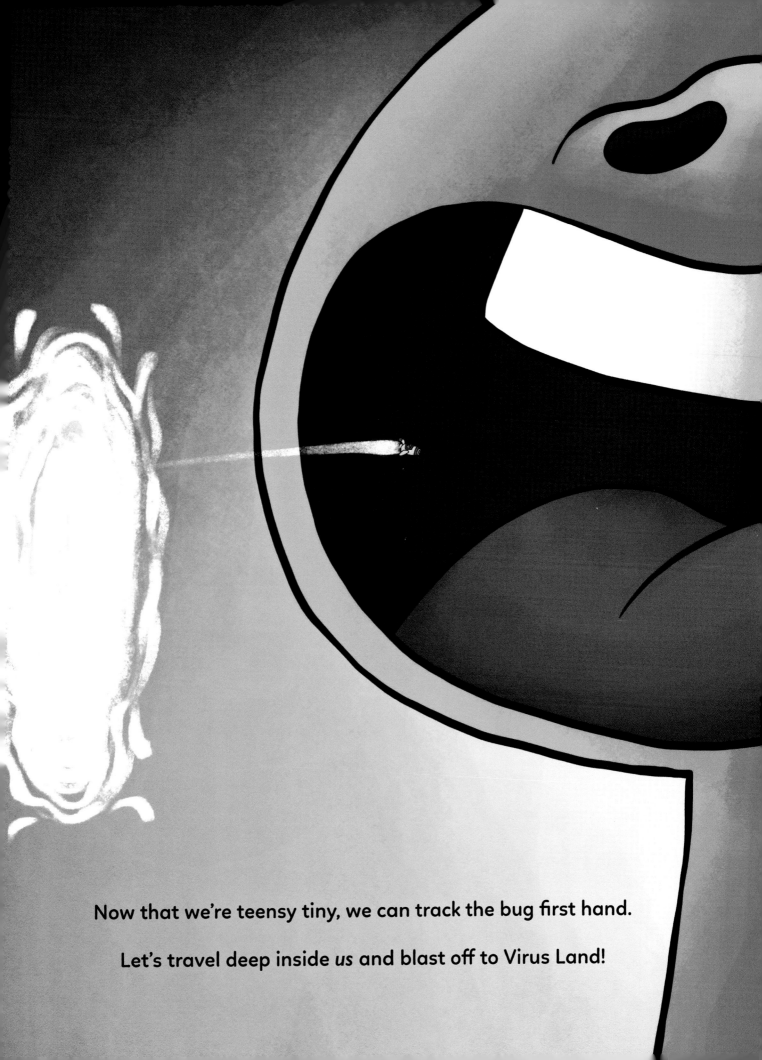

Now that we're teensy tiny, we can track the bug first hand.

Let's travel deep inside *us* and blast off to Virus Land!

We track it through the mouth.

Our rowdy ride has just begun!

We hear it hoot and holler

as it slip-n-slides the tongue.

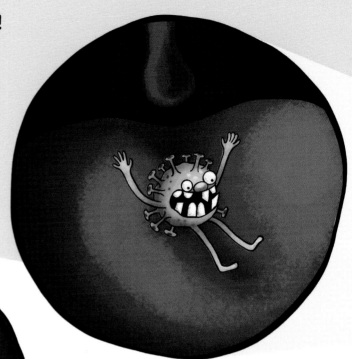

We sneak right past the voice box

where the human songs are sung.

This virus lingers deep within

the hollows of the lung.

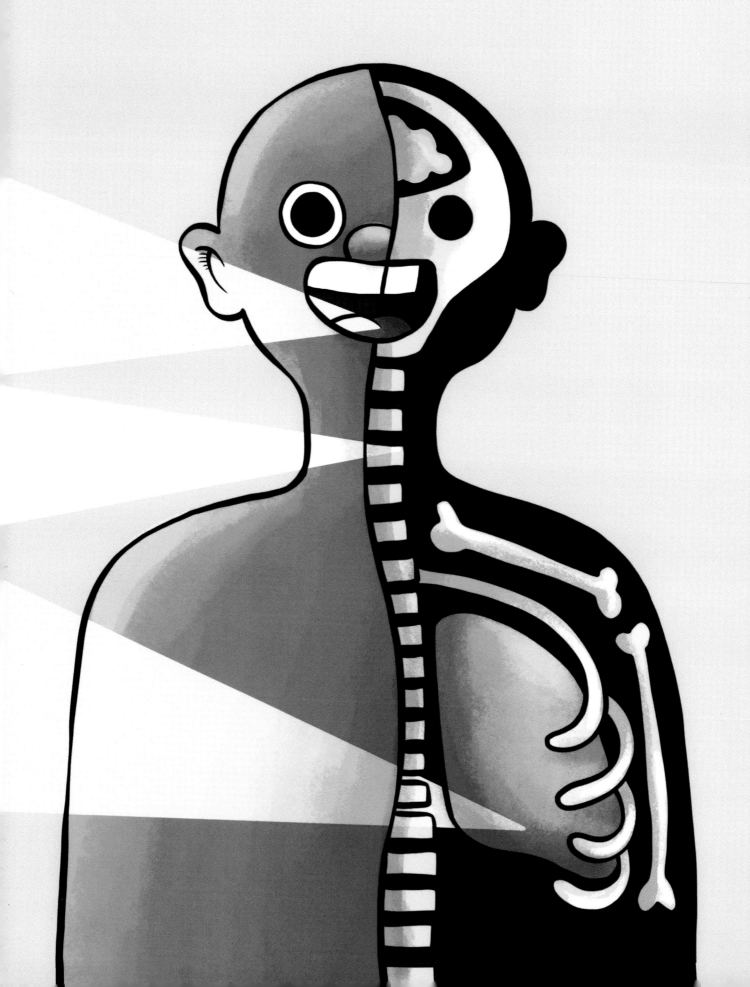

We find its cozy cave where it tells stories by the fire.

The flames begin to build - the body's temperature grows higher!

Sometimes it takes a week before a fever starts to show.

So if you have a fever, you should let somebody know!

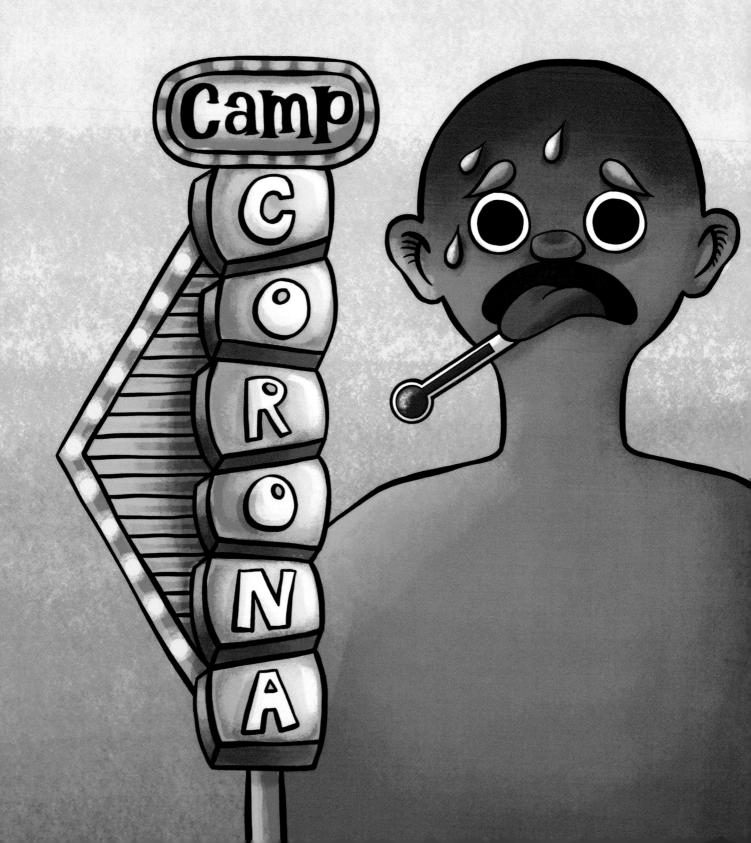

It practices dark magic tricks to cast an evil spell -

It sings up to the spirits as it steals your sense of smell!

The virus starts to dance a sickly dance within the chest.

The dancing makes you cough and want to lie in bed and rest.

The lung is only *one* place where the virus likes to play.

It sets sail down the bloodstream causing symptoms on the way.

No time to board the boat to enter human circulation.

Let's stick around the lungs to find out how it crossed the nation!

We grab hold of its cape as we fly up, up, and away!

We exit from the body in a snotty, sneezy spray.

The virus lies in wait atop the surface where it lands,

To board another human and cook up more virus plans.

Although this might sound scary, there's no reason you should fear.

By following these rules, you'll make the virus disappear!

**Rule #1:**
*"Cough into your elbow to keep the virus from spreading!"*

Avoid touching your face - it is a trap the virus throws!

Don't ever let it catch you with your finger up your nose!

**Rule #2:**

*"Try not to touch your face or rub your eyes!"*

Let's not forget your hands, which might just *look* sparkly and clean.

The germs are all around but they're so small they can't be seen.

**Rule #3:**
*"Wash your hands often with lots of soap
to send the virus swimming down the drain!"*

Keep all your buddies close but don't get closer than 6 feet.

Play games with all your friends but know this virus likes to cheat!

This bug will try to tag you even if you're out of reach.

A distance of 6 feet is the last rule that we will teach.

**Rule #5:**

*"Keep 6 feet of space from your neighbors!"*

With each and every virus, the best way to intervene

Is with powerful potion doctors give, called a vaccine.

All over planet Earth, scientists work to make this tool -

And you can join their team if you just study hard in school!

It's now time to go out and put your knowledge to the test.

You're ready for the mission! You're the best of all the best!

Gear up with a cool mask and a big smile across your face.

We'll beat this nasty bug and send it back to outer space!

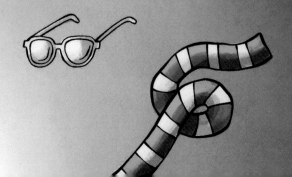

THE END.

# Glossary

**Antibody:** (noun) a part of the body's defense system against foreign invaders; more specifically, it is a protein produced by white blood cells that helps fight disease-causing agents, like coronavirus.

**Blood vessel:** (noun) a tubular structure that carries blood between the heart and the organs of the body; these include the arteries and veins.

**Disease:** (noun) a disorder of structure or function that has a specific set of symptoms, like COVID-19.

**Epicenter:** (noun) the focal point or geographic hotspot where there is the most disease activity.

**Epidemic:** (noun) a disease that is widely distributed within a community.

**Fatigue:** (noun) feeling tired; one of the symptoms of COVID-19.

**Fever:** (noun) an abnormally high body temperature that occurs as part of the body's response to a foreign invader, such as a virus.

**Infectious:** (adjective) capable of spreading; similar to 'contagious.'

**Inflammation:** (noun) a condition in which blood cells are recruited to an area of the body to help protect the body from foreign invaders or injury, often leading to the region becoming red, hot, swollen, and painful.

**Lungs:** (noun) a paired set of organs within the chest that allow a person to breathe by exchanging carbon dioxide for oxygen.

**Mutation:** (noun) a change within an organism that occurs between generations; more specifically, it is a change in genetic information and can occur in viruses when they multiply.

**Outbreak:** (noun) the abrupt or sudden occurrence of a disease within a population.

**Pandemic:** (noun) a disease that is widely distributed across the world.

**Symptom:** (noun) a feature or sign of a condition or disease.

**Transmit:** (verb) to pass on or spread a disease; similar to 'infect.'

**Vaccine:** (noun) a substance used to help protect the body from a disease; more specifically, it causes the body to produce proteins called antibodies that help provide immunity, or protection, against a particular disease.

**Virus:** (noun) a microscopic, infectious agent that can only multiply within the living cells of a host, such as a human.

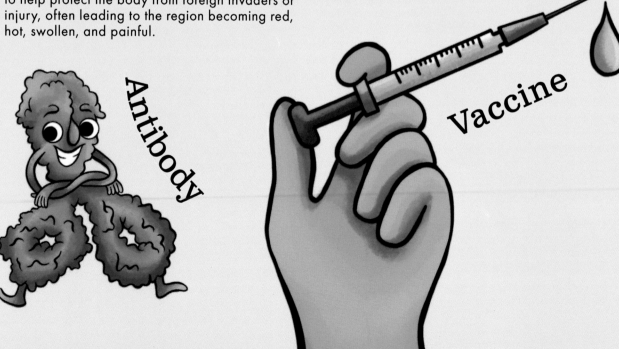

Antibody

Vaccine

# Coronavirus Disease 2019
# (COVID-19)

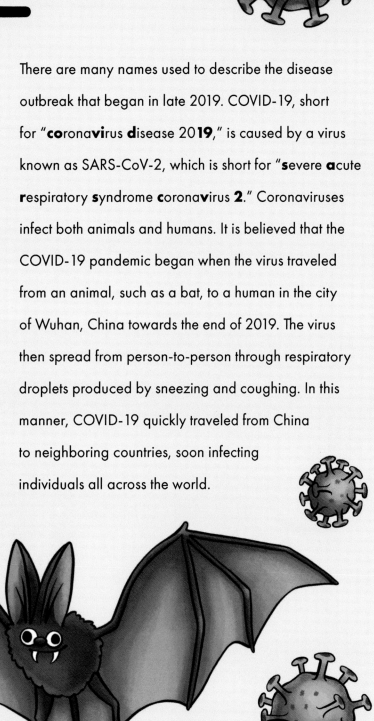

There are many names used to describe the disease outbreak that began in late 2019. COVID-19, short for "**co**rona**vi**rus **d**isease 20**19**," is caused by a virus known as SARS-CoV-2, which is short for "**s**evere **a**cute **r**espiratory **s**yndrome **c**orona**v**irus **2**." Coronaviruses infect both animals and humans. It is believed that the COVID-19 pandemic began when the virus traveled from an animal, such as a bat, to a human in the city of Wuhan, China towards the end of 2019. The virus then spread from person-to-person through respiratory droplets produced by sneezing and coughing. In this manner, COVID-19 quickly traveled from China to neighboring countries, soon infecting individuals all across the world.

# Tracking a

The Coronavirus Disease of 2019 began in the city of Wuhan in the province of Hubei, China. It quickly spread to regions all throughout the world. As viruses spread from person to person, their bodies can change in different ways. These changes are called **mutations**. Viruses like coronavirus often mutate in ways that help them spread more easily. However, these changes also typically cause a milder form of illness. Therefore, overtime viruses can become more infectious but less harmful.

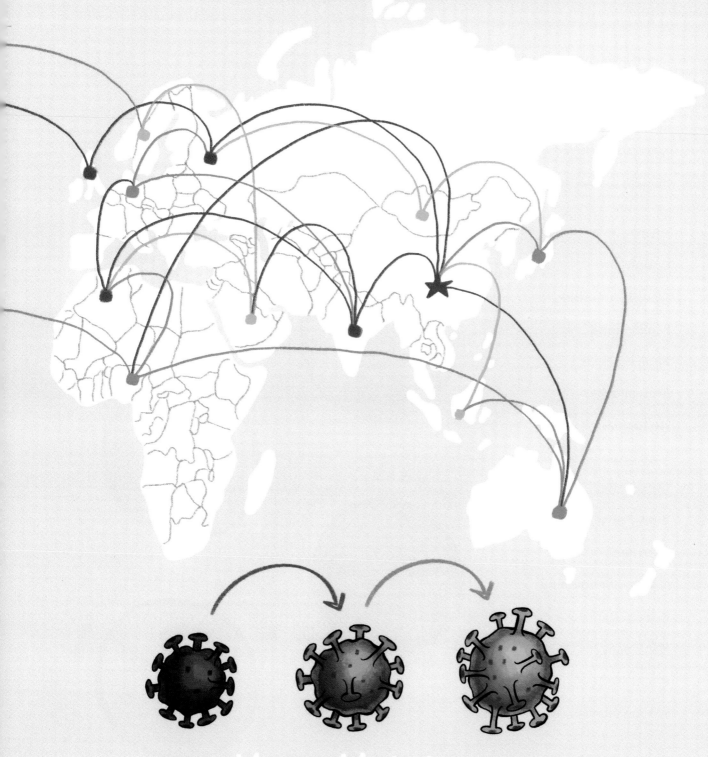

# Symptoms of COVID-19

The symptoms of COVID-19 vary in their onset and severity. They typically begin several days after a person is infected with the virus but can take upwards of 2 weeks. On the other hand, some people never feel any symptoms at all. Overall, children are less likely to get severely sick from COVID-19. However, certain symptoms are more likely to occur in children and may indicate a condition involving widespread inflammation, known as multisystem inflammatory syndrome in children (MIS-C). These symptoms are colored green below.

Fever

Cough

Trouble breathing

Feeling tired

Shaking chills

Muscle aches

Headache

Sore throat

Loss of smell or taste

Runny or stuffy nose

Diarrhea

Nausea or vomiting

Belly pain

Neck pain

Blood shot eyes

Feeling extra tired

Rash - especially on fingers and toes

Feeling extra tired

Neck pain

Belly pain

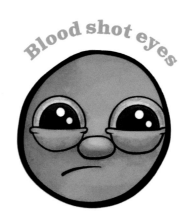

Blood shot eyes

Rash on fingers and toes

# The
# Human Body

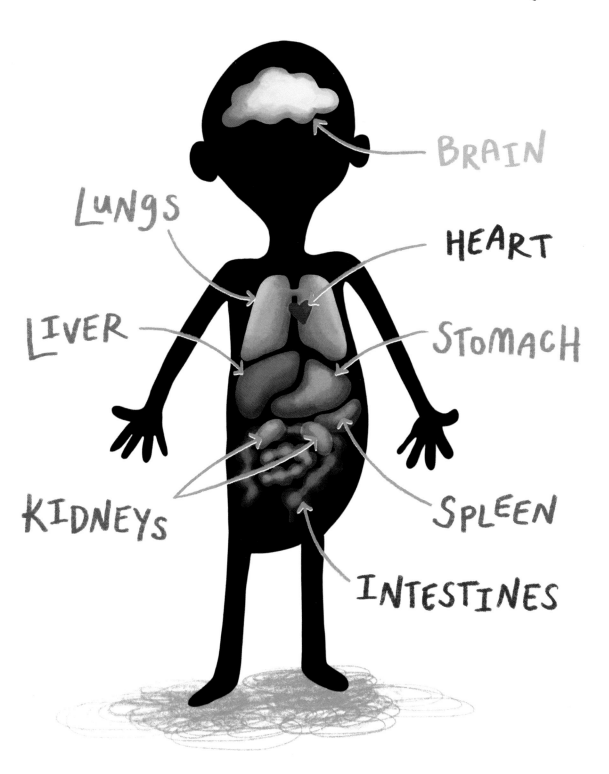

# How is the virus spread?

The virus enters the human body through the eyes, nose, and mouth. It can be spread before symptoms set in and all throughout the course of the illness. When you cough or sneeze, a misty spray leaves your mouth and remains floating in the air. This cloud contains tiny virus particles that can infect other people. Eventually the droplets in this cloud fall and settle on surfaces, where the virus can survive anywhere from hours to days depending on the material of the surface. Because humidity and air flow cause the droplets to fall much faster, it is important to socialize in outdoor settings.

# You Can Beat Coronavirus!

Contact your doctor if you have any questions or concerns.

# FACT VS FICTION

 **Did coronavirus come from outer space?**

No! It started in an animal species and then spread to humans.

 **Does the virus spread through droplets in the air?**

Yes! Be sure to wear a mask and keep 6 feet of space from your neighbors when possible.

 **Does coronavirus start a fire in your lungs?**

No! However, it **can** cause inflammation and an immune response throughout the body.

 **Does the virus dance in your chest?**

No! However, it **can** cause a cough & chest pain.

 **Does coronavirus use magic or spells?**

No! However, it **can** cause you to lose your sense of smell.

 **Can the virus be found in the lungs?**

Yes! Once it is in the bloodstream, it can travel all throughout the body.

 **Does maintaining 6 feet of space mean you can't see your friends?**

No! It is important to continue playing with your friends, as long as it is done in a safe manner.

 **Does catching COVID-19 mean you will have it for life?**

No! The virus can be eliminated from the body upon recovery.

 **Should UV radiation, bleach, methanol, or ethanol be used on your body to protect yourself from COVID-19?**

No! These substances are harmful to the human body and should not be used as a form of treatment or prevention.

 **Do most people who get COVID-19 recover from it?**

Yes! Most people who get COVID-19 have mild or moderate symptoms and recover with supportive care.

# Where can I learn more?

Because viruses evolve and new information is constantly discovered, it is important to stay up to date with the most current information. Check with your doctor or a public health official to get the most updated information about how to protect yourself from SARS-CoV-2.

If you would like to learn more about the COVID-19 pandemic, please visit:
1. United States Centers for Disease Control and Prevention (CDC) at www.cdc.gov/COVID19
2. World Health Organization (WHO) at www.who.int/emergencies/diseases/novel-coronavirus-2019

If you would like to learn more about your specific area and opportunities to help within your community, reach out to your town's Board of Health or your state's 'hotline' phone number.

If you have any questions or concerns regarding the informational content of this book, please direct them to your doctor.

Many people experience feelings of sadness, anxiety, or stress during times of health crises. If you are feeling down or depressed, reach out to a friend who can help! Call 1-800-662-HELP (4357) to access the National Helpline (SAMHSA) for free, confidential, 24/7 help.

*"During times of stress, it is important to eat healthfully, exercise regularly, and keep in contact with close friends and relatives. If you are feeling overwhelmed, try to focus on activities you enjoy and limit your amount of news intake per day."*

References

"Advice for the Public on COVID-19." World Health Organization, World Health Organization, www.who.int/emergencies/diseases/novel-coronavirus-2019/advice-for-public.

"Coronavirus Disease 2019 (COVID-19)." Centers for Disease Control and Prevention, Centers for Disease Control and Prevention, www.cdc.gov/coronavirus/2019-ncov/index.html.

Guan, Wei-jie, et al. "Clinical characteristics of coronavirus disease 2019 in China." New England journal of medicine 382.18 (2020): 1708-1720.

Lai, Chih-Cheng, et al. "Severe acute respiratory syndrome coronavirus 2 (SARS-CoV-2) and corona virus disease-2019 (COVID-19): the epidemic and the challenges." International journal of antimicrobial agents (2020): 105924.

Lauer, Stephen A., et al. "The incubation period of coronavirus disease 2019 (COVID-19) from publicly reported confirmed cases: estimation and application." Annals of internal medicine 172.9 (2020): 577-582.

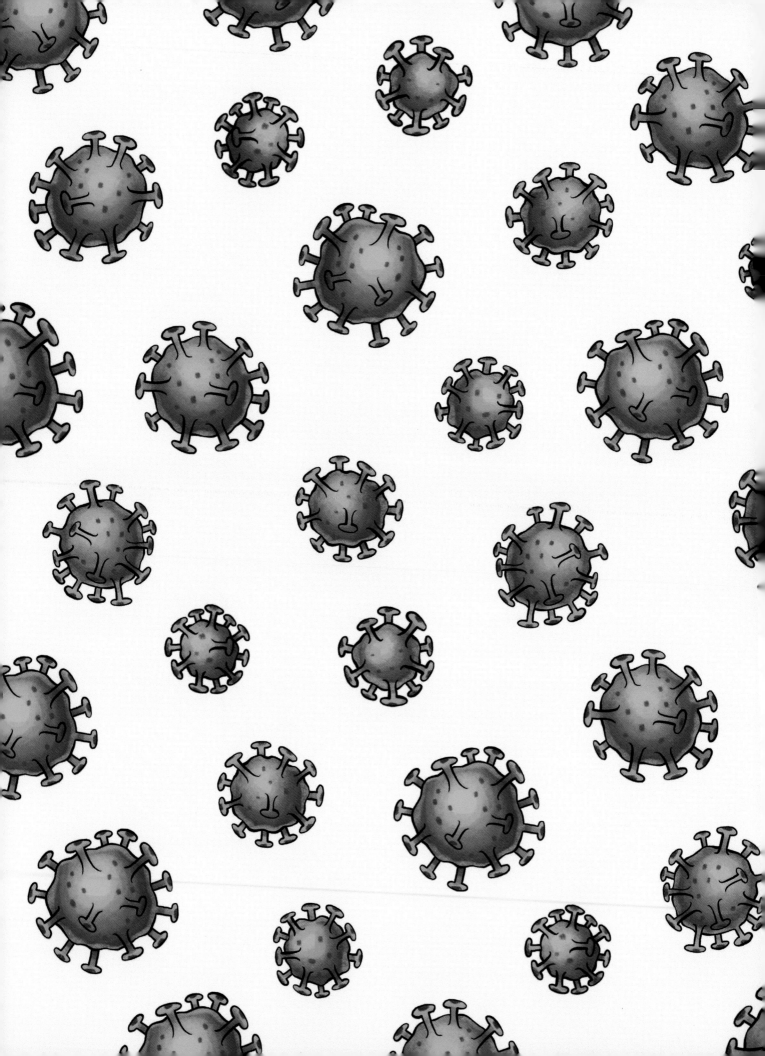